15.95

D1267060

Native North American Stories

Retold by Robert Hull
Illustrated by Richard Hook
and Claire Robinson

121886

THIS BOOK IS THE PROPERTY OF
MOUNTAIN REGIONAL LIBRARY
YOUNG HARRIS, GEORGIA 30582

Thomson Learning

New York

Tales From Around The World

African Stories
Native North American Stories

Editor: Catherine Ellis
Series Designer: Tracey Cottington
Book Designer: Derek Lee
Color artwork by Richard Hook
Black and white artwork by Claire Robinson
Map artwork on page 47 by Peter Bull

First published in the
United States in 1993 by
Thomson Learning
115 Fifth Avenue
New York, NY 10003

First published in 1992 by
Wayland (Publishers) Ltd
61 Western Road, Hove
East Sussex BN3 1JD, England

Copyright © 1992 Wayland (Publishers) Ltd
U.S. Revision Copyright © 1993 Thomson Learning

ISBN 1-56847-005-3

Cataloging-in-Publication Applied For.

Printed in Italy by G. Canale & C.S.p.A., Turin

Contents

Introduction

About 30,000 years ago, or perhaps earlier, some men, women and children started walking from the eastern end of Siberia over the thin footbridge of land that leads to what is now Alaska. It was a risky journey. They didn't know what to expect. They didn't know that the continent that we now call America was somewhere in front of them. But they went, and made new homes. More and more people traveled to Alaska and found places to live. Slowly the wandering peoples spread across thousands of miles of mountains and plains and rivers, and settled down in all the regions of North and South America.

These were the first people to live in America. There were, of course, many different groups, or nations, of people who lived all over the continent, and each nation had its own name: Blackfoot, Lakota, Seneca, Sioux, Cree, Crow, Navajo, Micmac, Iroquois, Susquehanna, Papago and a hundred more, all with their own languages and ways of life. There were hundreds of different languages and dialects all over North America, and an extra language used by the buffalo-hunting peoples – sign language.

Because of the different parts of the country they lived in these peoples came to have very different ways of life, and very different kinds of homes. The people of the northwest coast often had large decorated houses, with totem poles outside. The Inuit peoples of the far north built winter houses half underground, often with whale bones for rafters. In the summer they lived in tents made from seal or caribou skins. In the eastern woodlands and around the Great Lakes lived the Iroquois and Mohawk peoples, who were mostly farmers. Some lived in long wooden houses, others lived in wigwams. After horses were introduced to the Plains, people could hunt buffalo very successfully, and they became dependent on buffalo for food, clothing, some of their fuel, and even shelter. These Plains people lived in tepees – cone-shaped clusters of poles covered with buffalo skin – which were easy to move so the tribe could follow the buffalo. In the hot southwest, houses could be built of sun-dried mud bricks; and in the desert there were cliff dwellings, villages of houses built of stone or carved into the rock.

I like to imagine what went on in all these different kinds of homes. Especially how for hundreds, perhaps thousands, of years the people told each other stories. Nearly always after dark, when the work of the day was finished, in tepee and wigwam, in wooden house and stone dwelling, stories were told. Told, not read. There was no written-down language, and all the knowledge that a tribe or people needed, such as how to make medicines, was stored in people's memories, or recorded in the form of pictures, woven perhaps in cloth. The same with stories. They were remembered in people's heads, not on paper, and were told and re-told thousands of times. There were thousands of stories, and they were always being added to, and new ones invented.

Though everyone must have told stories at different times, there were storytellers too. In the pictures made by people of the southwest, they were shown with children crowding around them, sitting on their laps and their arms, and leaning over their shoulders. They told funny stories about the rascally adventures of Coyote or Hare, scary stories about ghosts, stories about how Raven or Glooscap or the sun made the world. Stories about why Beavers have big flat tails, about why wolves chase deer, about why there is death. Then there were some stories that were so sacred they were known only by a few members of a tribe.

For children and adults, the world was one huge book of stories. Here is just a page or two from that book.

Raven

*I*n the far northwest of America, among the Inuit peoples, Raven the Giant is a favorite character. He is Tul-ug-auk-uk, the creator of life, who came out of the first darkness.

The beginning of earth

At the beginning of time there was darkness. But in that darkness, there was already something else. It was Raven. He was very small, no bigger than a grain of corn, and did not know who he was.

Raven crouched down, listening. He heard nothing. There was no sound in the world, no bird calling, no river splashing. There was nothing but darkness in the world. Nothing could make sound. Except Raven, the small dark speck in the darkness. He moved, and his feathers made a tiny whisper. It was the first sound. He spoke a thin "craw." Another. He moved his wings. A strange thing happened when he moved them. The wings grew. He moved them again. They grew bigger each time he moved them. So he beat them and beat them to make them bigger. As he beat the darkness he felt it change. It became heavier. The darkness gradually became earth.

So solid earth came into being, beaten from the dark under Raven's wings, like iron in a smithy.

Now Raven knew he had power. He walked forward on the ground, beating his wings. As he moved forward

across the world, the first things came into being behind him, taking shape in the wake of his passing wings. The upward beat of his wings began the mountains, the downward beat the valleys. The valleys wound out behind him, and hills struggled up. He looked back, and could just make out the dim outline of his work in the darkness.

Raven went back over the world again. His wing struck hard against rock, and water sprang out. It was the first spring. He went on. Trees like enormous feathers grew up near the first river.

Raven climbed. He found himself on a high precipice, looking down. He tried to see what he had made. There was a dim faint glimmer along the river. He wanted to see. He stretched his wings wide, as if to grasp it all. He knew he had made it all. He thought, "I've made this!" And then, from peering down so long into the dark, he overbalanced and fell.

He stretched out his wings and they held him up. Raven flew with his wings.

He circled over the world and cried, "Crawk! Crawk!" "Crawk!" he cried with all the power his voice could make. "Crawk! Crawk!" the dark valley echoed. Raven knew from the sound of his voice that he was Tul-ug-auk-uk, the Raven creator, maker of everything that could be.

He flew into a tree and rested, thinking. Raven could imagine clearly what he had done, but he could not see it. It was dark across the world, with only frail glimmers of light among the dark cloud and mist that he had scattered about. He looked down from his tall tree, staring hard to see light.

At last he saw a glinting down by the river. He flew down and found a rock that was making a light. It had a small stone in it that flashed when he turned it. He gripped the rock in his claws and with his beak pried the stone out from it. He scratched off the hardest mud and light glowed upward from it. He rolled the glinting stone in the water at the river's edge and then rubbed at the rest of the mud with his feathers.

As the mud fell away there was an explosion of glaring light. It was as if all the dark in the world had left at once. Raven put one black wing over his eyes for a shield. He had found Sun.

Wrapping Sun in one of his own dark feathers, Raven flew up as high as he could and left Sun on top of the highest mountain. There Sun was far enough away and would not hurt Raven's eyes.

He flew to a tree and looked around. In the new light he could see. Raven could see everything he had created.

Coyote

In the stories of the Crow people, and other nations of the Great Plains, the Animal People were the first beings on earth. Coyote was the most cunning of them, and he was set to work by the Great Spirit Chief to finish making the world. Though Coyote is often a mischief-maker, he is also a hero and creator.

The creation of people

Coyote had nearly finished making the world ready. He had prepared the sky and the earth, and put things in their places. He had planted the forests and arranged the lakes. He had built high mountains and spread them with snow.

Then he made everything move. He whirled the mountain snow high in the air with his tail, threw the winds across the lakes, and pushed the waterfalls over cliffs. When the things on earth were in motion, Coyote sat back on his haunches and pointed his muzzle to the night sky. He began to howl and howl, and soon the stars and moon began to move across the night.

Wolf, Bear, Deer, Hawk, Sheep, Owl, Mouse and the other Animal People sat around with him, watching the stars move, and talking about the wonderful way he had improved the world. He liked listening to their praise and congratulations. Feeling pleased with himself, he said importantly, "I must go to sleep now. Tomorrow I have to make the New People."

9

Next morning he wished he hadn't told them, because they all wanted to help. As soon as first dawn crept into the sky in its gray fox-skin they started coming to him with their suggestions. They sat around in a circle to discuss things. Wolf said, "I think the New People should be able to howl very loudly so as to frighten everybody."

"Like you, you mean?" said Coyote.

"Yes," said Wolf. "They won't be able to manage without a good howl."

"I disagree," squeaked Mouse. "The New People should have a small squeak for a voice. That way they'll be able to talk to the others very privately."

"They won't want to have voices like either of you," Bear interrupted. "Wolf's voice would scare everyone away, and Mouse's wouldn't even be heard. No, the important thing for New People is to be able to stand

up on their two back legs and crush things flat. Like this." And Bear gave the air a frightening hug.

"The way you crush things," Coyote said, with a slight sneer.

"Well, of course," Bear replied.

Then it was Beaver's turn. "I don't know why you're making such a fuss about unimportant things when you've not even talked about tails. The New People should have very big flat tails, to be able to slap the water loudly and build dams with."

"The New People will build dams like yours?" Coyote asked.

"There are no other kind," Beaver said with a sniff.

And so it went on. Owl and Deer and Fox and Cougar and Falcon and the rest all thought the New People should be like themselves, with very sharp ears or a curved beak or whatever it was they prided themselves on. In the end Coyote got fed up. "Look," he said, "you all want the New People to be just like yourselves. What's the point of that? If they howl like Wolf and have big teeth they might as well carry the name Wolf and be Wolf. But we want them to be different, and we want to tell them from the rest of us. I suggest we all make a model and see whose is the best, and the best will be the New People."

There was some quiet snarling and hooting, but in the end each of the Animal People agreed to make a model of the New People from the mud by the river. "Remember," Coyote said, "you had some good ideas. Bear said the New People should be able to go on two legs. That was a good idea, because then they'll be able to reach into the trees for food. Deer was right saying they should have sharp eyes and ears. That was good. But one thing you didn't say, which is very important. The New People must be cleverer and more cunning than any of you."

"Like you, you mean?" they all chorused.

"Well, yes," Coyote said.

13

That evening, instead of talking in a circle again, all the Animal People took water and mud from the river and made models of New People. Mouse made small ones with long thin tails. Owl made them with wings and big round eyes. Hawk's New People had sharp curved beaks. Bear's had long sharp claws.

Coyote made Man and Woman.

Coyote had finished his models, but he still had important things to do. That night, while the exhausted animals slept, Coyote took water from the river, and poured it over all the models the animals had made. The wings of the owl, the beak of the hawk, the claws of the bear, were all washed away. There were only the models of Coyote's New People, Man and Woman, left lying on the forest floor near the river. Then, by the small light of the stars moving overhead, Coyote knelt beside his motionless New People, and slowly into the nostrils of Man and Woman he sent breath, and they began to breathe.

At dawn the animals woke to find the New People standing at the river's edge, looking out at the world with thoughtful eyes.

14

Thunder

For many Native American peoples, like the Pawnee and the Blackfoot on the Great Plains, and the Tlingit and Kwakiutl of the northwest, Thunder was sacred and dangerous. Thunder has always brought life-giving rain in his storm clouds, but at first he wanted human life in return. As in this story, he was a huge bird who sometimes preyed on creatures of the earth.

Thunderbird

At the beginning, Thunder descended from above the sky to the earth. He paused on the summit of a mountain, and unfurled his black robe. The first dark clouds rolled across the empty blue sky and into the valleys. Thunder guided them with his shouting. As he went, his loud voice went everywhere among the hills. His fierce glances went down to the earth with a crackling fire. Storms of rain fell, grass and trees sprang into being. The earth was clothed in wind and cloud.

And so it went on.

Thunder decided that for his traveling over high mountains and the endless plains and oceans he would take wings. He changed his nature, and became a huge creature, Thunderbird. Thunderbird built a lodge on the cloudy roof of the world, in the highest cedar. From there he could swoop down to the ocean, snatch a

whale in his talons, and soar with it into the clouds. As Thunderbird soared above the world, or dived down for prey, his huge slow wing-beats made thunder, and as his eyes searched the earth lightning flashed and crackled from his beak.

The first people feared Thunderbird. They heard him everywhere. They heard his wing-beats far out on the prairie. They saw his lightning hit the rock and break it to pieces. They found smoking trees that he had split apart. They saw people struck to the ground, never to rise again. But after the dry time of winter, the people needed Thunderbird to come with his storm clouds. They knew they had to put up with the deafening wing-beats passing close overhead, and the lightning from his beak striking jaggedly at the earth. Each year they prayed for him to bring the great rain to refresh the land. Each year, at the same time, they listened for him. Each year, when flowers came to the woods, Thunderbird returned.

The people watched the first storm of spring climbing the hills, and saw its downpour standing near them on the river bank, and they were glad. Even though they were afraid when Thunderbird was nearby flapping among the storm clouds, they knew that after the rain the crops would rise again.

As well as fear, however, there was great sadness for the first people at springtime. Thunderbird demanded a sacrifice in return for bringing his storms to them. He would not leave them in peace; he would not fly back to his high lodge until they had chosen a young woman to sacrifice to him. Every year he took a young woman away with him to his lodge. He was powerful, and they could not defy him.

It made the first people endlessly unhappy, having to decide whose daughter they should choose for

Thunderbird. Finally one year, after talking for many days, they decided that they would no longer sacrifice anyone's daughter. Some of the people said that Thunderbird would be furious and destroy their village, some said there would be no more dark clouds and rain to make the crops grow. But after everyone had spoken the people agreed to defy Thunderbird for the first time. No young woman was brought from her house for Thunderbird to take away.

As soon as Thunderbird saw their disobedience, his blackest fury broke right over their village. For the whole day he terrified them with his anger. No one had ever experienced anything like the din he made, continuously wheeling and flapping right over them. No one had ever seen such fierce light sizzling around them. The people's tallest tree was split down the middle, and the smell of a burning hut filled the air. But the first people did not give in.

Suddenly, the sky cleared. A few people thought Thunderbird had given in to them and gone. They came out of their houses to sit in the evening sun. Others weren't sure; they believed that Thunderbird would take a young woman by force if they refused to give him one.

Then Thunderbird struck. He came over the edge of the mountain, out of the clear blue sky, and with a grim flash of lightning struck a man down to the earth. The man's young wife screamed and ran forward, and as she did so, Thunderbird swooped back low over the ground, snatched her up in his talons, and with a great shout and clap of wings was gone as quickly as he had come, leaving only a fading rumble in the distance.

After a while the man who had been struck to the ground stood up and looked vaguely about him. He was dazed. Then he saw that his wife had gone. He knew that Thunderbird must have taken her to his cedar lodge above the clouds. The man brooded for many days alone, thinking of his stolen wife. Most of the time he sat motionless in his house or at the river's edge. He went out in his canoe one day to think. He realized that if he went to find his wife, no one would come with him. No one would defy Thunderbird a second time.

17

He decided to make the journey. He would try to find her. She was at Thunderbird's lodge, somewhere above the clouds, in the highest mountains. He knew she was there. But how could he find Thunderbird's lodge? How could he ever find the way there? How, he wondered, could he rescue his wife from the talons of Thunderbird even if he did find the lodge?

He didn't know the answer to any of these questions, but he set out anyway. He asked all the animals he met, Bear and Beaver, Owl and Coyote, but none of them had seen her or knew where Thunderbird's lodge was. "He is the creature we fear most. We would never journey to his lodge. We run when we hear him coming," they told him.

All through the summer and into the autumn the man wandered among the mountains searching. When he had almost given up hope of finding Thunderbird's lodge he met Raven, watching out over a valley from just outside his lodge. When the young man told Raven his story, Raven invited him inside the lodge and gave him food.

"So, Thunderbird has stolen your wife?" Raven said. "Well, I know where Thunderbird's lodge is. It is close to mine, on this very mountain, just above us in the clouds. His lodge is a dreadful place that no one should want to visit. But you have every reason to want to go there and face Thunderbird. It is lucky that you saw me, for there is only one creature whom Thunderbird cannot kill, only one creature he fears. It is I, Raven. If you have powerful medicine from me you can confront Thunderbird in his lodge."

Raven gave him a glistening black feather.

"Take this. Go to Thunderbird and tell him why you have come. When he threatens you, point this feather at him. He will not be able to attack you. Then take this black arrow made from elkhorn, and shoot it through the wall of his lodge. If you can do that, your wife will come back with you."

The man set off up the mountainside. Following a track that led up into swirling cloud, he soon came upon the tangle of wooden sticks that was the gate of the cloudy cedar lodge of Thunderbird.

He pushed it to one side and went through the stone entrance. It was dark inside. The man spoke boldly into the echoing dark, "I have come to return my wife to the world of people."

There was silence, then a rustling metal noise as Thunderbird stepped forward.

"What foolish creature dares invade my lodge? Creatures die who enter here unasked." A flicker of jagged lightning spilled from his beak and illuminated the lodge.

THIS BOOK IS THE PROPERTY OF
MOUNTAIN REGIONAL LIBRARY
YOUNG HARRIS, GEORGIA 30582

12/88b

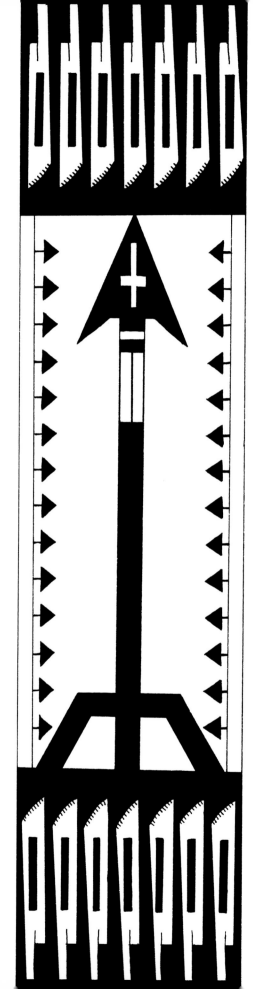

But meeting Raven had given the man strength to face Thunderbird. "You have stolen my wife. I have come to take her away."

Thunderbird came forward to strike. The young man pointed Raven's black feather toward him. Thunderbird fell back. Then the man fitted Raven's black elkhorn arrow to the bow, drew it, and shot it first time through the wall of the lodge. There was a splintering crack and sunlight flooded in. Thunderbird was beaten.

"You have strong medicine. I respect you. I must give your wife back to you, but first you must listen to me. I am the great power of the spring. I shall still live in this cedar lodge among the clouds. I shall stay here until the birds fly south, and then go with them. You have found great power and defied me. When I return again with my storm clouds I shall no longer descend and demand a young woman from the people. There will be no sacrifice. Instead you will give me your prayers. You will smoke your prayers up to me in the sky.

"I shall give you my pipe to take back to your people. When it is the time for me to come with the rain storms and begin the spring again, you must fill this and smoke it in the evening, and let the breath of its smoke rise into the sky. It will tell me that you remember Thunderbird who brings the spring storms and the warm rains that ripen the berries and sweeten the grass. Remember me with your songs and with the smoke of this pipe, so that I do not need to come from the sky to take sacrifice from you."

Thunderbird gave the man his sacred medicine pipe, and took him down to the mountain trail again. As the swirling clouds and mist parted, the man saw his wife already standing there, her black hair glistening in the sunlight. They embraced, and looked at each other with renewed love. They were happy to have each other again, and as they started back down the mountain, they were happy to be carrying the medicine pipe to the people, knowing that from now on Thunderbird would be content with the prayers that rose from it.

From that day Thunderbird no longer took young women from the first people. He is still feared, but he keeps to his places in the sky, returning each day to his cedar mountain lodge in the clouds.

22

Why Wolves Chase Deer

*A*nyone who hears the cries of wolves deep in the forest might guess that, as they follow each other through the dark, they enjoy sending their voices echoing and ringing up to the stars. They do. But they also enjoy coming to the end of their travels, and sitting around the fire listening to each other's stories. This is a story from the Tsimshian people on the coast of British Columbia.

One day all the wolves met in a forest clearing at the edge of a river to talk and sing stories. Wolves have always liked boasting, and many of them wanted to sing about their travels and adventures, telling how they climbed the highest mountains, or went for days without food.

At the end of the day they all sang together about what it was like being wolves. They sang about the forests and the snowy mountains and the cold rivers. They sang about long winters and finding food for small wolves. The cubs joined in, and the long howling of their song filled the whole river valley with sound.

The night was full of such a continuous howling that the other creatures fled from it. Mole burrowed straight underground, and some of the tinier creatures ran under stones and stayed there. Fish flattened themselves to the bottom of the river, and have been flat ever since. The salmon were so alarmed they sped along the river and, when they came to rocks, hurled themselves uphill towards the mountain tops. It was the

first time, so they say, that the salmon leapt up through the rapids and waterfalls.

The moon was the only creature who liked the endless chorus of the wolves. She came out to walk among the tops of the pine trees and stood above the clearing listening for most of the night. Looking down she could see her own light on the fangs of the wolves as they threw back their heads to sing even more loudly. It was a great feast of wolf stories. The singing went on till the mists rose before dawn.

The mists carried the wolves' voices winding through the forest to the ears of the deer. The deer didn't recognize the sound, but they were curious, and so they came down to the river to see who these creatures were. When the deer met to tell their own stories they barked quietly to each other, and they thought the wolves' echoing, howling voices were the strangest they had ever heard. And because of that, and because they just didn't believe some of the wolves' tales, they started to whisper among themselves and ask who these creatures were. The whispering turned to sniggering and finally the deer started laughing out loud.

This didn't please the wolves at all. They looked across the river and glared at the deer, who by now were laughing continuously, and couldn't stop. It would have been better for the deer if they had, or if they had gone away and laughed quietly among themselves. But they didn't. They were bigger than the wolves and had no fear of them.

After a while the wolves, who had been staring back at the deer in annoyance at such insulting behavior, saw that the deer's mouths, which were wide-open laughing, had no large glinting fangs in them. They knew for the first time that the large creatures called deer could not defend themselves. They would make perfect prey. The wolves in a pack surged across the river. The deer fled.

To this day the deer are running and the wolves follow them.

Winter and Spring

A story from the Iroquois people of the eastern woodlands.

Old Man Winter, Gau-wi-di-ne, built his lodge at the foot of a huge mountain. He surrounded it with mist and cold. High on the mountain above gathered the clouds that carry snow and hail. Stores of ice were piled deep on the mountain sides.

The old man's lodge was made of huge blocks of ice. Inside he stored his wood and frozen meat and fish. He cooked them over his fire, a fire that could not warm him, however much wood he put on, however high its flames leapt. He was Old Man Winter, Gau-wi-di-ne, and could not be warmed by a small fire.

No warm-blooded creature came to the lodge where snow storms blotted out the sky and the winds rang with cold. He was alone. No bird or animal or human being could enter, except his one friend, North Wind.

It was not often that North Wind came. He was too busy dragging the smoking snow from the mountain tops and driving it through the long forests, hiding people's trails and whitening their lodges. Sometimes he got lost in the storms he made, and strayed from his familiar haunts. Sometimes he spilled the snow he had been carrying before he meant to; then he had to return for advice from Gau-wi-di-ne, and gather more cold from the mountain.

He would call without warning. There would be the shake of his blundering step on the mountain and then a high-pitched scream, "uug-hwee-ee-ee, uug-hwee-ee-ee," and the old man's door would thump open as North Wind came swirling in with a freezing breath of snow. Down he sat by the fire, to smoke a pipe and take a rest from his endless journeying around the world.

On one of these visits, Gau-wi-di-ne and North Wind sat dozing and tired in front of the fire that gave them no warmth. As usual, the old man's beard was hung with icicles and his eyebrows were furry with frost, but tonight the icicles were less heavy, the frost less thick. The fire flared up higher than usual, throwing a glitter of light over his icy face. The old man's stiff white arm thrashed at the leaping fire, and an icicle fell from him and slid over the floor.

North Wind was alarmed. "Some warmth is here. What warm thing comes to threaten your strong lodge of ice and drive me away?"

"No warmth comes here," said the old man. "My lodge is strong. Have no fear. Go on your way again."

North Wind went out onto the mountain. A sudden fear came and he fled up the mountainside. His small fears followed him, sending the falling snow spinning about and pulling it down from the branches of the fir trees.

Near dawn, in his lodge, the old man heard a knock on the door. "Some foolish breath of North Wind," he thought. But the knocking went on, and became louder and stronger.

"I wish to enter the lodge of Old Man Winter," a voice said.

"Who dares to ask such a thing?" the old man shouted. "Go away! Only North Wind enters here! No other small creeping wind can enter." But as he was speaking the door swung open of its own accord. A handsome young man stood there. The fire flared up again and threw a light like a summer sunset over his face. As he stepped forward to meet Gau-wi-di-ne some of the snow that covered the old man's head and shoulders slid to the floor and melted. He greeted the old man and went over to the fire, putting out his hands to warm them. There was a glow of warmth and summery light in the lodge.

27

The old man was angry. "How dare you force your way in here against my wishes?" he said. "Go. Go at once. You are young, I do not want you by my old man's fire. You do not belong here. Your young breath is warm and will melt my lodge. I have banished warmth for ever under the long wastes of snow. It cannot return. Your eyes glimmer with the light of summer stars, and here that cannot be, for I sent North Wind to blow out the summer starlight long ago."

The young man merely smiled and went on sitting by the fire, only asking if he could fill Gau-wi-di-ne's pipe for him. The old man didn't answer, but went raging on.

"Do not underestimate me. I am powerful. I send North Wind all over the earth and at the sound of his voice its rivers come to a halt. I touch the sky and the snows hurry down. I lay my hand on the lakes and they become like fields of stone. I darken the sky and make the hunters crouch by their lodge fires and the animals slink to their caves. When I walk over the land it becomes hard as rock. You shine and smile like the sun, young warrior, but whenever I come the sun grows pale and flees far to the southland. I shall drive his glance from your face, and throw winter shadows there. Leave now, or I shall wrap your shining young limbs in freezing cold and turn them to mist and ice."

But the young man went on listening calmly and did not move. The old man began again. "You smile and do not fear me. Then listen: I am Gau-wi-di-ne, Winter himself. Now, fear me and depart. Pass out from my lodge into the cold winds."

The young man was unmoved. He filled the old man's pipe again, and then spoke, quietly and courteously. "Take your pipe and smoke, it will comfort and strengthen you for a while longer. But now you must smoke for me, for youth and Spring! I am young and strong, while you are old and slow. Can you not hear the voice of Ga-oh, South Wind? Your North Wind has heard it, and is already hurrying towards his northern home. You now, follow him to your lodge in the far north sky. Follow him before Ga-oh comes to warm the earth about this lodge. Your lodge here will fall. Your time has gone. Now is my time, and I am powerful." Against his will, the old man was listening.

"When I spread my hands, the sky opens wide and wakes the sleeping sun. I send my South Wind, Ga-oh, like a plow to turn the snow under the earth. I touch the earth and it grows gentle. I release the waiting buds into the air and let the impatient streams run freely in the sunlight. The trees hear my voice and reach out towards me. My breezes wander into the warming forest. I send down showers that whisper in the grasses, saying to them it is time to grow high. All this is my power, and now it is my time to rule the earth."

The old man was tired. With his pipe in his hands, he watched the young man anxiously.

"I came to smoke with you in peace and tell you all these things. Now the sun is waiting for me to open its door. You and North Wind built your lodge strong, but each wind, the North, the East, the West, and the South, has its time. Now South Wind is coming. Return to your lodge in the north sky. Go now in safety, before the falling arrows of the sun search you out."

The old man trembled. He seemed smaller, faded. In a thin voice he asked, "Young man, who are you?"

In a voice that breathed as soft as the breath of wild blossoms, the young man answered, "I am Go-hay, Spring! I have come to build my lodge on the green earth. I have talked to your mountain and it has heard. Its snows have already departed and its mists are making way for the sun. The sun is near. North Wind has fled. Now you must go, before it is too late. You have already waited long enough, and soon your white track to the far north will have disappeared." And as he spoke he threw open the door of the lodge. Light flooded in, and Go-hay began singing the sun song. For Gau-wi-di-ne it was time to leave. Off he went, hurrying along the fading trail northwards.

Where the lodge of Old Man Winter had been, shoots of flowers were already pushing up their green tips. The stream that had been frozen ran spiraling and glittering through the new grass. A bluebird sang nearby, and another answered further off.

Only on the summit of the mountain was there a hint that Gau-wi-di-ne had once been there, a curved sliver of snow on a north-facing ledge that waited there like something forgotten.

Gau-wi-di-ne had ended his time, and Go-hay ruled the earth!

Bluebird and Coyote

A story from the Pima people of the southwest.

Bluebird was once Graybird, a dull, dirty-colored bird that no one looked at. One day he discovered a lake of bright blue water. He flew down to the edge. "Perhaps if I go in the blue water," he thought, "I shall become the color of the lake." He walked about for a while, and then dipped his head in the water and took it out to look at his reflection. No good. He was still a boring dirty-colored gray bird.

Just then, he saw Butterfly resting on a rock. Butterfly was exactly the color of the lake. "Where did you get that color?" Graybird asked. "I bet it was the lake."

"That's right, it was," said Butterfly. "Why?"

"Well, I'd like to be the same color as you," Graybird said. "How can I do that?"

"Well," said Butterfly, "if you want to be blue like the lake, you have to do what I say. Listen. You bathe in it four times every morning for four mornings, facing the four directions. You sing a song asking the lake for some of its beauty – 'Blue lake, blue as the cloudless sky, give me some of your color for my dull feathers,' – or something like that. Then, if you're successful, you thank the lake with another song. Until you do that you mustn't touch anything, otherwise your new blue color will disappear."

Graybird obeyed all the instructions, and after the

fourth day he was the same blue as the lake. He stretched a wing out sideways to have a look at his new color and was delighted. Then he made up a thanking song and sang it. After that he went flitting about and stopping to cock his head on one side and look at himself in every pool of rainwater he came to. He thought how beautiful he was. And so Graybird became Bluebird.

One morning a few days later Coyote came along and saw Bluebird preening himself at the lake's edge. Coyote thought how splendid Bluebird looked. He immediately decided he would like to be the same color. A coat of blue fur! That's what he wanted! So he asked Bluebird where he found the beautiful blue for his feather coat, and Bluebird told him. He gave Coyote the same instructions that Butterfly had given him.

Well, Coyote followed the instructions and did everything right. On the fourth morning he came out looking terribly handsome. He said aloud, "Now they'll call me Blue Coyote." He looked down at his blue shadow, then turned around and around several times looking at his blue tail and haunches. Then off he trotted to find a pool of rainwater and admire himself properly.

Coyote was so pleased with himself he forgot to compose a song thanking the lake. He soon came to a pool and peered in and thought how gorgeous he was now.

"What a stylish nose," he thought. "What irresistible ears." He looked this way and that, twisting about for a look at all of himself. He would soon be telling every creature he met: "I was gray you know," and enjoying their astonishment.

He couldn't wait, so off he dashed down the trail, glancing around every now and then at his gorgeous coat, and turning sideways to watch his fine blue shadow trotting alongside him. Ke-runck! He ran flat into a tree. He'd not been looking where he was going. He rolled in the dust and howled. There was mud and dust all over his new fur. He brushed and brushed at the dust and he was still dusty. His new blue self was nowhere to be seen. He couldn't believe his eyes. He'd forgotten his thanking song to the lake.

That's why Coyote is the dusty color he is today.

The First Love Music

Among some peoples, like the Lakota Sioux who lived near the Missouri River in what is now Nebraska, the flute was for love music. Its sound was believed to be like the call of an elk, and the elk was important in love. If a man put an elk footprint on a small mirror and flashed the sun's rays from it into a girl's eyes, she would fall in love with him. A flute had the same kind of power. The flute player, like Orpheus or the Pied Piper, could sometimes draw people magically to him.

One spring day long ago a young Sioux hunter was following the trail of an elk. He was keen and alert, but elk are hard creatures to get close to. They are shy and slip away at the least disturbance, and they're very fast runners. On this particular day the young hunter found tracking elk especially difficult. He had followed a faint trail for hours, without ever seeing the creature itself, and now he was growing anxious. The herds would be leaving for the high summer pastures in the hills. If this one escaped, who knows when he would find another. His people needed elk meat; they were hungry.

There was another reason why the young Sioux was worried. He was in love, and the elk, the swiftest and wisest of the animals, carries the best love charm. If the hunter possesses elk medicine, the girl he is in love with will fall in love with him too. He needed a strong charm, because many other young hunters wanted her. She was beautiful, and the chief's daughter too.

Now, the tracks of the elk had finally led him into some woodland. He could tell, looking closely at the fresh prints, that the elk was nearby somewhere. It was walking too, not running. Perhaps it had stopped to feed. He was excited. But though he crept silently through the woodland, peering this way and that under the trees, he saw nothing. He was just about to give up when he saw it, a huge handsome elk stretching up to feed on some birch shoots. He dropped to the ground and stalked very slowly on his knees over the grass. Five minutes later he was within shooting distance. He drew his bow. Screwing up his eyes to focus he watched the elk over the flint of the arrowhead, and was about to let the arrow fly when the animal turned, sniffed the air, looked toward him, then bounded away through the bushes.

The hunter knew this was the last he would see of the elk. His day's hunting was over. He was utterly weary, all the more so because he hadn't been successful, and because he had to go so far to get back to his village. He now had to find the trail again. In his excitement at following the elk through the woodland, he hadn't memorized his path. He tried this way and that, but the only tracks were other deer tracks, and he just couldn't find a way out. It was getting dark.

When night came, and there was no moon, he realized he was totally lost. The best thing he could do would be to wait till dawn. He would easily find his way out of the wood by daylight. He had a little dried meat, and he could hear the trickle of a stream. He found it, drank some cool water, wrapped his fur blanket around him, and lay under a tree to sleep.

Now, although the young hunter knew the ways of the open plains, he didn't know the forest. He had no idea how noisy it was by night. He was used to sleeping out in the open plain, under the quiet stars. Here in the forest sleep was impossible. There was the endless whispering of the leaves, even when there was no breeze. Then the wind had only to rise a little, and the trees began groaning and creaking, as if they were wringing their hands, he thought. As creatures of the night passed close by there was the crack of a twig, a slight splash as something went though the stream. All night long animals called to each other. The forest was full of screeches and warblings and howls and churrings. What a creepy place!

After that he must have dozed for a while, because he was suddenly conscious of a new sound. It was a strange, eerie humming, a vague sound that rose and faded like the breeze he had heard earlier. It scared him. It could have been a spirit sound, the roaming voice of a ghost. He shivered, and pulled his robe closer. There it was again, this time more persistent, yet still wavering and hesitating. It couldn't be a hurt spirit, it was too calm. As he grew used to it, he became less fearful. He thought the sound was beautiful and haunting. It was like a song. It made him remember waking up one misty summer dawn on the plain, and of an afternoon drifting downriver in his

canoe, and of other beautiful things. And of course it made him think of the girl he loved.

It even sent him back to sleep. In his sleep he had a dream. In the dream Wagnuka, the red-headed woodpecker, was sitting on a branch above him, singing the song he had just heard. It was singing, "Follow me, follow me, follow my trail to find the song."

The song woke him up. The sun was already streaming through the misty branches, and the forest was a din of noise. Above him was Wagnuka, the red-headed woodpecker, just as in the dream. It flew off a little way. Remembering the "follow me" in the dream, the young hunter gathered his things together and followed it. Wagnuka flew to another tree, and waited there. Then, the hunter heard the song again, but there was something very strange about it, and different from in the dream. He realized it was not Wagnuka singing. Something else was making the sound Wagnuka had made in the dream. He was puzzled.

The bird flew on ahead. Again he followed it. It settled on a cedar tree, and began hammering at a dead branch, with a noise like a small drum. As the young hunter watched and listened, a sudden breeze surged through the trees. The sound he had heard in the night came with it. It sighed momentarily and faded. The sound, the same strange floating, sighing sound he'd heard in the dream, had come from the dead branch Wagnuka had just been drumming on. What was it? The breeze rose and fell again, and this time he knew that the ghostly sighing he had heard was the air blowing through the holes the woodpecker had made in the branch.

The young hunter decided he would take this new music home. The tree didn't need the branch, and Wagnuka could soon drill another one full of holes. But he apologized to the tree as he broke the branch off carefully and put it under his arm.

The sun had been up for a while by now, and the young hunter had no difficulty finding his way out of the forest. He walked all day, carrying his cedar branch under his arm, and at evening came to his village. He had brought back no meat, and no elk medicine to make the girl he loved love him. But he had a secret

music. An invention, a different sound. His people would soon have a beautiful new sound for the sacred dances, to go with the drums and the rattles and the bull-roarers. The girl he loved might like the sound.

It seemed a wonderful idea, but try as he might he couldn't make the new music come from the branch. He sat alone at night in his tepee and tried all kinds of ways to get the branch to sing again. He waved it hard in the air. He blew across it. He wondered if it was the night air it needed, and went outside. Nothing would make it speak again. He wondered if the wind that sang over the rocks would do it. He went out to a high rock and held the branch for the wind to blow across it naturally. But nothing he did made the song return.

The young hunter was very unhappy. He purified himself in the sweat lodge, and went out at night to the rock. For several days he stayed away from the village, praying and fasting, praying for a vision to come to him of how the music was made. It worked. A vision did come, in another dream. Wagnuka, the red-headed woodpecker, visited him in the shape of a man, with a small branch of cedarwood. "I am Wagnuka, come to show you how to make the branch sing. Watch carefully what I do."

In his dream he watched, and saw what to do. Next morning he went to a cedar tree that grew just inside the forest. He broke off a small branch, and made it hollow, using the bowstring drill men and women use to make smoking pipes with. He made holes all along it, as Wagnuka does with a dead branch. He gave one end the shape of a bird's head, and painted it red. He made a small fire of sage and cedar and let the smoke drift through the music pipe, along the throat and out at the beak. He went again to the foot of the cedar and prayed.

Then, in front of the cedar, he took up the pipe and lowered his mouth sideways to the wood. With his mouth almost closed, so the breath came out in a steady flow, he blew gently across the mouthpiece, lifting a finger from each of the holes in turn, listening with his eyes closed. It came! There it was! There was the gentle sound he had heard, the ghostly music of the swaying cedar.

40

They say that at the beginning the Great Maker gave each of the trees a voice of its own. Now it was the new voice of the cedar flute that drifted from the forest edge across to the village, and people stopped to listen. They had not heard this music before. They went to see where it came from, and found the young hunter sitting under the tree. He had hunted a new music. He had given them the first flute, the siyotanka.

Every day the young hunter listened to himself making songs. He had heard old people say it was Hasjelti, the Bringer of Dawn, and his brother Hostjoghon, the Twilight Bringer, who made all the great songs of the world. So he would play at dawn outside his tepee, and the songs he found seemed to take their wavering mistiness from the mists on the river, and the quickly glittering twisting tunes seemed to glint like early sun on the cool water. Then he would play at the foot of the cedar in the evening, and as the songs drifted over the village, they made the evening calmer, and the stars seemed to come closer to listen.

He could not stop playing. His music grew better and better. People said his songs were inspired, and they were. But it was not just the dawn and the twilight that made his songs so full of longing, but the daughter of the chief of the village. She was more difficult than the music. She was happy to be by herself, and very proud.

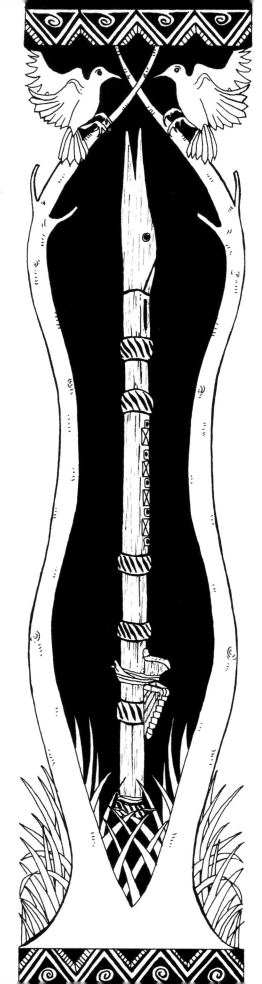

She didn't want anything to do with any of the young men who came to court her.

The young man's only hope, he knew, was his music. He decided he would make a special love song for her, a charm of sounds to make her love him. He listened again for many nights and days to all the sounds of the earth, to bird song in the woods, to the whisper of grasses, to thundering waterfalls. Then he made a song. One evening, he stood under a tree near her tepee, and played the music he had made for her. Soon, drifting across the air was the most beautiful music his flute had spoken, sad, tender, hopeful, and full of the things of the earth.

She heard it. She was sitting with her family around the fire in the tepee. They were comfortable in the warmth, and she was eating delicious buffalo meat. But the song of the siyotanka set her feet moving, and soon her feet wanted to move in the slow dreamy dance of the song. The music was too strong to be resisted, and it drew her outside into the night.

She would have been content just to listen, but her feet said, "Go nearer." They took her nearer to the sound. She saw the young man's shape in the shadow, she saw the outline of the flute. She intended only to stand and listen, but as she listened her feet said, "Go to him and thank him." She went to him. She intended to stand a little way from him and say only her thanks, but her feet said, "Go up to him." She went close and looked at him. Without intending to she said she loved him.

And so, because of the music of the siyotanka, the young hunter and the chief's young daughter came to love each other. Their two families agreed that they should live together.

The young men of the village, once they knew about the new music magic, immediately started making their own flutes, shaping branches of cedarwood into hollow pipes. They made them like the one the young hunter had made, in the shape of a bird's head with a long neck and an open beak. At first their love music was awkward, but gradually it became as haunting and magical as the music of the first flute, and the new love music traveled from village to village.

42

Death and Heaven

The sky is important in Native American stories, the moon and stars as well as the sun. To the Skidi Pawnee people of Nebraska, the misty stretch of stars that we call the Milky Way was also a road, or way. It was the long white road across the sky which spirits traveled when they left the earth for their new home, the Last Hunting Ground – so-called because they believed there was always plenty of game to hunt. Other peoples thought of the white road of these stars as a river of white water.

The last journey

It was the summer's end, the time when sadness crosses the land in lengthening shadows from the mountains, and thistledown floats along the rivers.

Wahu had been a fine hunter. He had always caught enough food for his family, and never been wearied by the endless trails over the mountains or the long cold days on the river. But his strength was leaving him. He could not hunt as he used to. Now, except for his dog, Wahu was alone. His wife had died, and his children lived in distant valleys and villages with their own families. He didn't have the strength to visit them again.

He would talk to his dog sometimes, but mainly Wahu spoke with the long shadows, and the voices that came to him from the mists that hung in the valley in the evening. The voices came to him from times that

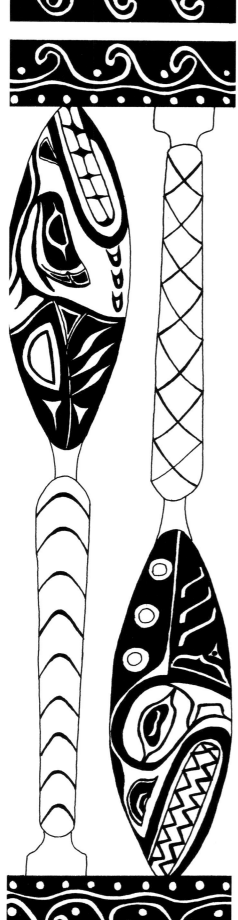

had passed, from the dear ones who had gone, and the close friends of his childhood.

Wahu could no longer take an interest in the present, and knew that it would soon be time for him to begin his last journey. He made ready his canoe. He took out his worn paddle, splintered from the many rocks the water had surged around in his youth.

He thought of the times he had made the journey with friends. He could almost hear their laughter on the water. He thought of the dawns and sunsets he had seen on the river. He remembered the times he'd seen elk standing at the water's edge, and the salmon that had leapt glimmering by him. This was a journey he would make alone, without friends or laughter, and he would not stop to fish, or to make camp and wait for the next dawn to rise.

It was time to begin. He pushed off in the early morning from the small beach where he had always moored his canoe, and looked around once, to see the sun shining in the pine-tops over the clearing where he had built his lodge long ago, and down through the coiling river-mist where he drifted now.

The water was still and dark.

He could see no fish. Behind him, his dog stood in the shallows, waiting for the canoe to turn around and come back to fetch her. Instead, there was only the wave of Wahu's arm as the canoe slowly moved out of sight.

For hours the trail of the canoe made a long calm 'V' on the water. The sun rose to its noon height, then fell slowly across the long afternoon. The shadows lengthened and the air became cool. Wahu would soon be able to hear the thunder of the white water. He had never been this far, but he had heard of the white water that foamed and spilled between high rocks. The sound foretold the end of his journey.

The tall rocks came into sight. They were at the entrance to the road to the Last Hunting Ground. Here he had to pause. He drove his canoe gently into the shallows. Two shadowy figures stepped forward.

"Are you alone?" said one. "It is sad to travel to the Last Hunting Ground unaccompanied."

"I am alone," said Wahu.

But he was not. His dog had followed him all the way, sometimes swimming behind the canoe, sometimes following the trail as it wound along the bank. At that moment she pulled herself out of the water, and shook herself. She trotted over and jumped into the canoe. The shadowy figures pushed them off, toward the white water. They had no need for a paddle now. The spirits would keep the canoe riding clear of the rocks, until they were into the Long White Water of the Sky, drifting toward the Last Hunting Ground.

Notes

Blackfoot   (p. 15)
The Blackfoot people lived on the western plains and mountains. They got their name from the black-dyed moccasins they wore. Blackfoot communities still live in northern Montana and southern Alberta.

Coyote   (p. 9-14, 33-4)
Sometimes called Old Man Coyote, Coyote was a favorite among many Native American peoples, especially those of the Great Plains. He is a two-sided character, being both a tricky and untrustworthy scamp, and a hero who performs great feats to help the people. For instance, he stole fire from the Fire People, and filled the rivers with salmon. He also helped create the world.

Crow   (p. 9)
The name of a people of the northern Plains. Their name for themselves means Bird People, but can also mean the bird crow.

Elk   (p. 35, 37)
Elk are the most splendid members of the deer family. They are shy, and can run fast – about 30 mph. They go to high mountain pastures in the summer and come down to the plains in winter. Some peoples believed that if a man gave elk medicine to the girl he loved, she would fall in love with him.

Four Directions   (p. 32)
The four directions were always honored by Native American peoples. East, north, west and south were given names and totem animals. Many dwellings, the tepee for instance, had an opening toward the east.

Gau-wi-di-ne   (p. 26-31)
This is the Iroquois name for Old Man Winter.

Go-hay   (p. 31)
Go-hay is the Iroquois name for the youthful Spring.

Inuit (say In-you-it)   (p. 4, 6)
Inuit is the name used for the Native American peoples of the far north, from Alaska to Greenland. There are many different nations of Inuit people.

Iroquois (say Ear'-oh-kwah)   (p. 4, 26)
The word Iroquois comes from an Abenaki word meaning "Real Snakes." Their traditional lands are in the eastern woodlands – what is present-day New York State. They were some of the peoples whom the first European settlers met, and they include the Cayuga, Mohawk, Oneida, Onondaga, Seneca and Tuscarora peoples, as well as many others. Today there are Iroquois people living on thirteen reservations and reserves in New York State, Quebec, Ontario and Wisconsin.

Kwakiutl (say Kwah-ke'-yut-ul)   (p. 15)
The Kwakiutl live on the northwest Pacific coast.

Long White Water in the Sky   (p. 43, 45)
This is one of the names given to the dense stretch of stars we call the Milky Way. The Navajo call it the Rainbow Bridge.

Medicine   (p. 20, 22, 35)
To the Native North American peoples, anything can be medicine if it has been given strength or power, or been made sacred. Medicine can heal, but it is also used for other things, as in the story about Thunderbird.

Music   (p. 35, 40-42)
Music is important to Native American peoples. They have drums, rattles made from gourds, bull-roarers and flutes. A bull-roarer is a feather-shaped piece of wood which makes a loud whizzing-humming sound when it is whirled on a string. Flutes were sometimes used for sacred dances and for love music. Some people believed they helped to lure animals close when hunting.

Pawnee (say Paw-nee')   (p. 43)
The Pawnee were Plains people. Their name means "Horn." They call themselves this because of the men's traditional hairstyle. They shave the hair from the sides of their heads and then use buffalo grease to make the hair on top stand up

NATIVE NORTH AMERICA

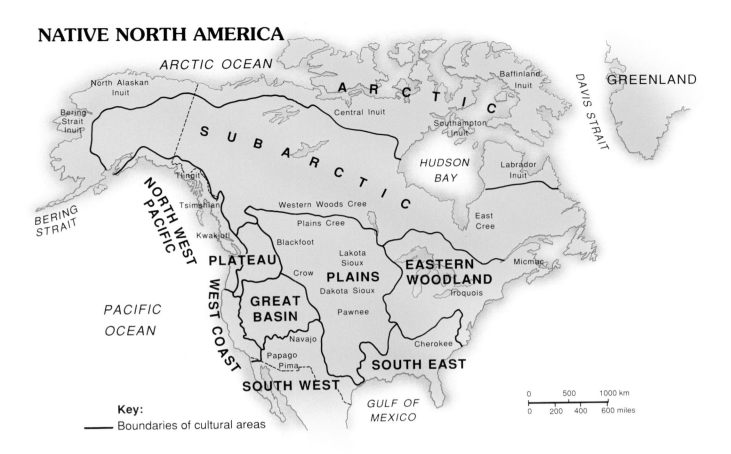

Key:
——— Boundaries of cultural areas

like a horn. The Pawnee were farmers and skillful buffalo hunters. Today there are four groups of Pawnee living in southern Oklahoma.

Pima (say Pe'-ma)   (p. 32)
The Pima lived in what is now Arizona. They were farmers who grew corn, cotton, tobacco and other crops.

The Plains   (p. 5, 9, 15)
The rolling prairies and grasslands that lie between the Mississippi valley and the Rocky Mountains are known as the Great Plains. Many different nations of Native Americans lived here – the Blackfoot, Cheyenne, Pawnee, Comanche and Apache. After horses were introduced in the nineteenth century, buffalo-hunting became central to the Plains peoples' way of life.

Raven   (p. 6-7, 20)
Like Coyote, Raven is both a creator and a trickster. The Native Americans of the northwest thought of Raven as maker of the world, and

bringer of light. He provided people with fire, and stole salmon for them from the Beaver People who, at the beginning of the world, kept the salmon all for themselves in one lake.

Sioux (say Su)   (p. 35)
The Sioux people lived on the Great Plains and are what many people think of as typical Native Americans: they lived in tepees, hunted buffalo, rode horses and wore feathered headdresses. Some Sioux leaders have became famous all over the world; you may know their names: Crazy Horse, Red Cloud and Sitting Bull.

Sweat lodge   (p. 40)
The sweat lodge is a small dome-shaped shelter made of saplings, where stones are heated in a fire and then water is poured over them. The steam that rises from the stones cleanses and purifies the bodies of those having a "sweat." People went to the sweat lodge before important events, like marriage. The idea was to be close to the warm center of the earth, and be cleansed in body and spirit.

47

Thunderbird   (p. 15-22)
Thunderbird is an enormous bird whose wing beats make the sound of thunder, and whose beak crackles with lightning. Small thunderbirds go with him, and their sound follows after him.
Thunderbird brings the storms of spring, and so helps the crops to grow. Some Native North Americans, such as certain Pawnee people, believe the voice of Thunderbird is what originally brought the world to life.

Tepee   (p. 5,, 40, 41, 42)
Tepees are the cone-shaped dwellings that many peoples of the Plains lived in. Tepees have frames of poles with buffalo-hide stretched over them, with a flap for an entrance facing east. They were often beautifully painted.

Tlingit (say Klin'-kit)   (p. 15)
The Tlingit people lived on the northwest Pacific coast, in what is now British Columbia.

Totem poles   (p. 4)
Totem poles are only used by people of the northwest. They are columns of wood with figures carved on them, usually animals. Each carved creature or sign means something: the moon

stands for high rank, the grizzly bear for fierce power. Each family has its own totem animal, so in any village there were totems of bears, beavers, deer and so on. Visitors to a village could go to the house that had the same totem as their own at home and expect a welcome. Totem poles are often tall (about 50 feet high), and brilliantly painted.

Tsimshian (say Shim'-she-un)   (p. 23)
The Tsimshian come from the northwest Pacific coast. Their main food source was salmon from the sea, and they had many ceremonies to show respect for and give thanks to the ocean and the salmon. Today a small community of Tsimshian live in southeast Alaska, and others live further south along the Canadian coast.

Tul-ug-auk-uk   (p. 6-7)
This is the Inuit peoples' name for Raven.

Wigwam (say wig'-wom)   (p. 5)
Wigwams are similar to tepees, but are generally smaller. Most are cone-shaped, but some are mound-shaped. They are made of poles covered with rush mats and bark. The nations in the east built wigwams.

Further Reading

Baker, Olaf. *Where the Buffaloes Begin.* New York: F. Warne, 1981

Baylor, Byrd. *A God On Every Mountain Top.* New York: Scribner, 1981

Brown, Dee Alexander. *Tepee Tales of the American Indian.* New York: Holt, Rinehart and Winston, 1979

Bruchac, Joseph. *Iroquois Stories.* Trumansburg, NY: Crossing Press, 1985

Connolly, James E. *Why The Possum's Tail is Bare, and other North American Indian Nature Tales.* Owings Mills, Md.: Stemmer House, 1985

Cook-Lynn, Elizabeth. *The Power of Horses and Other Stories.* New York: Arcade, 1992

Cunningham, Maggi. *The Cherokee Tale-Teller.* Minneapolis, Mn.: Dillon Press, 1978

Curry, Jane. *Back in the Beforetime.* New York: M.K. McElderry Books, 1987

Curtis, Edward. *The Girl Who Married a Ghost.* New York: Four Winds Press, 1978

Cushing, Frank Hamilton, compiler. *Zuni Folk Tales.* New York: Knopf, 1976

Erdoes, Richard, compiler. *The Sound of Flutes and other Indian Legends.* New York: Pantheon Books, 1976

Grinnell, George Bird. *Pawnee, Blackfoot, and Cheyenne.* New York: Scribner, 1961

Lewis, Richard. *All of You Was Singing.* New York: Atheneum, 1992

Matson, Emerson N., compiler. *Legends of the Great Chiefs.* Nashville, Tn.: T. Nelson, 1972

Monroe, Jean Guard. *They Dance in the Sky.* Boston: Houghton Mifflin, 1987

Yellow Robe, Rosebud. *Tonweya and the Eagles, and other Lakota Indian Tales.* New York: Dial Press, 1979